This Walker book
belongs to:

For Julie and for Alison

First published 2014 by Walker Books Ltd
87 Vauxhall Walk, London SE11 5HJ

This edition published 2015

2 4 6 8 10 9 7 5 3 1

This book has been typeset in Godlike

Printed in China

British Library Cataloguing in Publication Data:
a catalogue record for this book is available
from the British Library

ISBN 978-1-4063-6106-3

www.walker.co.uk

FSC
www.fsc.org
MIX
Paper from
responsible sources
FSC® C101537

WALKER BOOKS
AND SUBSIDIARIES
LONDON · BOSTON · SYDNEY · AUCKLAND

MINE!

Sue Heap

Once there was a little girl called Amy.

She loved her blankie very much.
"Mine," she said.
"My blankie. Mine."

Amy also loved her bear

and her bunny and her bird.

"Mine," said Amy.

Amy snuggled on her blankie
with Bear, Bunny and Bird.
"I love you all," she said,
"because we're together,
and because
you're MINE."

In came the twins.
"Can we play?" they said.
Zak picked up Bear and
Jack picked up Bunny.
And they whirled
them round
and round.

"Stop it!" Amy said.
"They're my toys,
my bear,
my bunny.
MINE!"

Zak and Jack played on.

Amy grabbed Bear and Bunny.
Zak and Jack grabbed back.
Then everyone shouted,

"MINE!

MINE!

MINE!"

Amy took her toys.
"NOT yours!" she said. "Mine!"

"Bird," said a little voice.
It was Baby Joe. In his hands
he held Bird, all teeny,
tiny and fluffy.

"Tweet!" went Bird as Baby Joe
squeezed it
and kissed it
again
and again.
Amy took Bird
from Baby Joe.
"MINE," she said firmly.

Baby Joe looked ever so,
ever so sad.

"He's all alone," said Zak.
"Without a toy," said Jack.

Amy looked at Bear.
She looked at Bunny.
She looked at Bird.

Amy knew what to do.

She gave Bird to Baby Joe.
"Mine AND yours,"
she said.
Then she let
Jack and
Zak hold
Bunny
and Bear ...

and everyone shouted,

"Yours
AND
mine!"